Can you find these bugs?

14 honeybees

1 tarantula

12 fire ants

7 Christmas beetles

4 praying mantises

TWIG

For Saxon, whose curiosity and
love of insects inspired this book

SIMON & SCHUSTER BOOKS FOR YOUNG READERS

An imprint of Simon & Schuster Children's Publishing Division

1230 Avenue of the Americas, New York, New York 10020

Copyright © 2016 by Aura Parker

First published in Australia in 2016 by Scholastic Australia Pty Limited

This edition published under license from Scholastic Australia Pty Limited

First US edition 2018

SIMON & SCHUSTER BOOKS FOR YOUNG READERS is a trademark of Simon & Schuster, Inc.

For information about special discounts for bulk purchases, please contact Simon & Schuster

Special Sales at 1-866-506-1949 or business@simonandschuster.com.

The Simon & Schuster Speakers Bureau can bring authors to your live event.

For more information or to book an event, contact the Simon & Schuster Speakers Bureau

at 1-866-248-3049 or visit our website at www.simonspeakers.com.

The text for this book was set in Quimby.

The illustrations for this book were rendered in watercolor, colored pencils, and artline pens

on watercolor paper with digital composition.

Manufactured in China

0418 SCP

10 9 8 7 6 5 4 3 2 1

CIP data for this book is available from the Library of Congress.

ISBN 978-1-5344-2468-5

ISBN 978-1-5344-2469-2 (eBook)

TWIG

Aura Parker

Simon & Schuster Books for Young Readers
New York London Toronto Sydney New Delhi

Bug School was abuzz with hundreds of shiny, scurrying shapes.

BUG SCHOOL

But not one bug noticed the new girl, Heidi,
tall and long like the twig of a tree.

Heidi waved hello to everyone.
But her teacher didn't even look up
from her looping and threading.

Scarlett and the spiderlings didn't see her.

Nor did the cockroach twins

or the stinky bug

or little Midge.

Miss Orb was a golden silk weaver
and a web-spinning champion.

"Good morning, class," she said
as she hung up her weaving . . .

on the

HAT STAND.

"Now let's begin our
counting lesson," she said.

One, two, three.

One, two, three.

I'm not a hat stand,

can't you see?

Heidi stood as still and straight as a twig.

The classroom was a flurry
of counting and color.

But nobody
noticed Heidi.

Nobody saw her
at lunchtime.

Nobody saw her here . . .

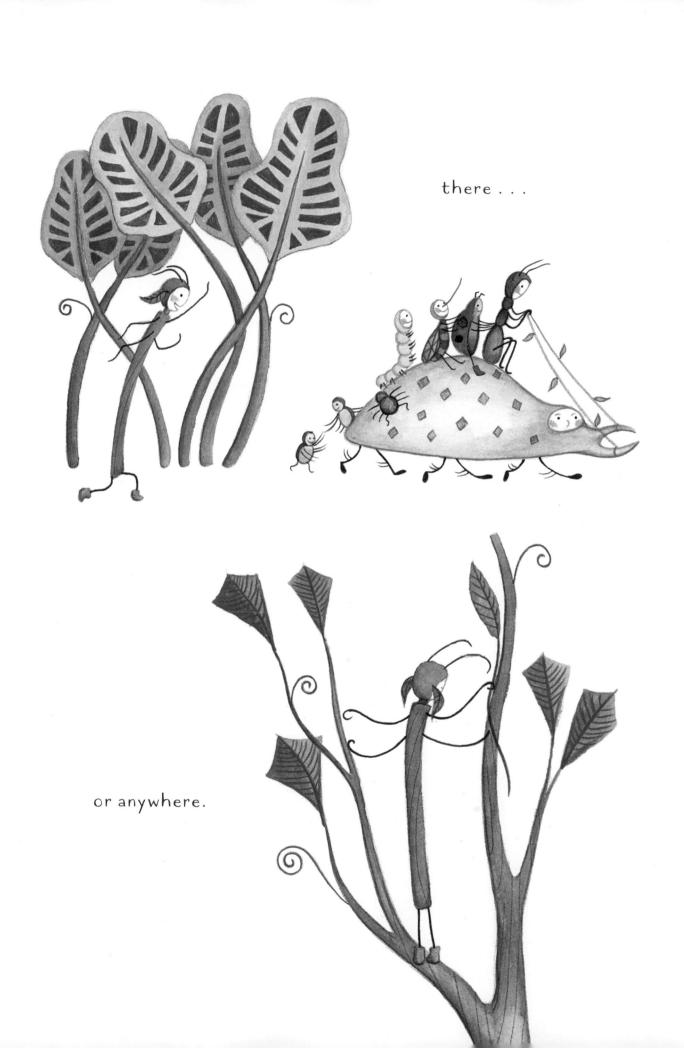

there . . .

or anywhere.

Nobody noticed Heidi at all.

One, two, three.

One, two, three.

'Why won't someone

play with me?

Miss Orb loved teaching everybody how to weave.
Weaving was tricky, with

sticky,

fiddly

threads.

Midge needed a little bit of help
from the cockroach twins.

The spiderlings did really well.

The stinky bug made
a present for Nana.

And Scarlett found lots of
things to add to her weaving.

An interesting leaf,

a piece of bark shaped like a heart,

 a blue crackly pebble,

 and a sprinkle of dirt.

Then she found a twig.

The twig let out a surprised yelp.

"I'm NOT a twig!

I'm me! I'm Heidi!"

And for the very first time, everyone saw her.
"Oops," said Scarlett. "You look so much like a twig!"
"Oh, there you are, Heidi!" said Miss Orb. "It seems your camouflage has been working *too* well!"

Midge just stared, for he could
hardly believe it.

Miss Orb had a wonderful idea.

"Let's welcome Heidi to our class by weaving her a scarf. Everybody can make a square and we'll sew them together. Then, we'll be able to see her wherever she is!"

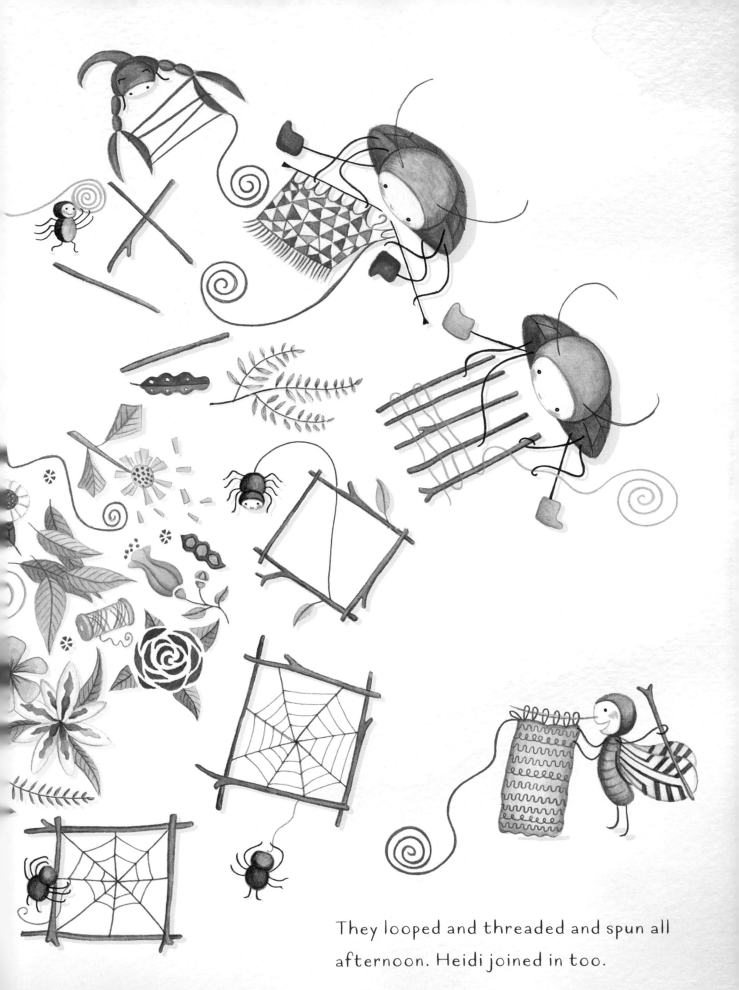

They looped and threaded and spun all afternoon. Heidi joined in too.

It was the best weaving they
had ever done.

Heidi smiled and spun and twirled.
She loved her new scarf . . .

and everyone could see
how happy she was.

These days, Heidi
always finds friends
in the playground.

She takes care of gaps when
they go on adventures.

Heidi helps reach things up high.

She even discovered a talent for basketball!

And Heidi always wears her scarf, except when it's time to play . . .

her favorite game,

hide-and-seek.

Can you find these bugs?

6 red-back spiders

2 cocoons

1 caterpillar

1 moth

18 leaf insects

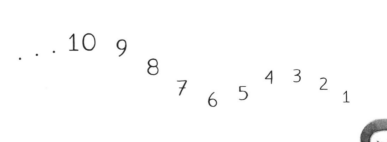

. . . 10 9 8 7 6 5 4 3 2 1